D0468548

Freedom Bird

WRITTEN BY
Jerdine Nolen

ILLUSTRATED BY
James E. Ransome

A Paula Wiseman Book
SIMON & SCHUSTER BOOKS FOR YOUNG READERS
New York   London   Toronto   Sydney   New Delhi

For Virginia Hamilton and the dream when it is set free
—*J. N.*

For my uncle and aunt, Joe and Shirley Ransome
—*J. E. R.*

SIMON & SCHUSTER BOOKS FOR YOUNG READERS
An imprint of Simon & Schuster Children's Publishing Division
1230 Avenue of the Americas, New York, New York 10020
Text copyright © 2020 by Jerdine Nolen
Illustrations copyright © 2020 by James E. Ransome
SIMON & SCHUSTER BOOKS FOR YOUNG READERS is a trademark of Simon & Schuster, Inc.
For information about special discounts for bulk purchases, please contact Simon & Schuster Special Sales
at 1-866-506-1949 or business@simonandschuster.com.
The Simon & Schuster Speakers Bureau can bring authors to your live event.
For more information or to book an event, contact the Simon & Schuster Speakers Bureau
at 1-866-248-3049 or visit our website at www.simonspeakers.com.
Book design by Laurent Linn
The text for this book was set in Chaparral Pro.
Manufactured in China
1019 SCP
First Edition
10 9 8 7 6 5 4 3 2 1
Names: Nolen, Jerdine, author. | Ransome, James E., illustrator.
Title: Freedom bird / Jerdine Nolen ; illustrated by James E. Ransome.
Description: New York: Simon & Schuster Books for Young Readers, [2020] | "A Paula Wiseman book." |
Summary: In the antebellum South, two siblings shelter a large, mysterious, wounded bird and eventually
follow it west toward freedom.
Identifiers: LCCN 2018039878| ISBN 9780689871672 (hardcover) | ISBN 9781481402224 (eBook)
Subjects: | CYAC: Fugitive slaves—Fiction. | Slavery—Fiction. | Freedom—Fiction. | African Americans—Fiction.
Classification: LCC PZ7.N723 Fr 2019 | DDC [E]—dc23 LC record available at https://lccn.loc.gov/2018039878

Sometimes, on account of what those who have come before us do with their lives, a pattern in the world forms like the lines in a quilt that repeat over and over. And those actions continue to shape the lives of children and their posterity. Maybe it is that way with you and yours. Well, it was that way with John and Millicent Wheeler.

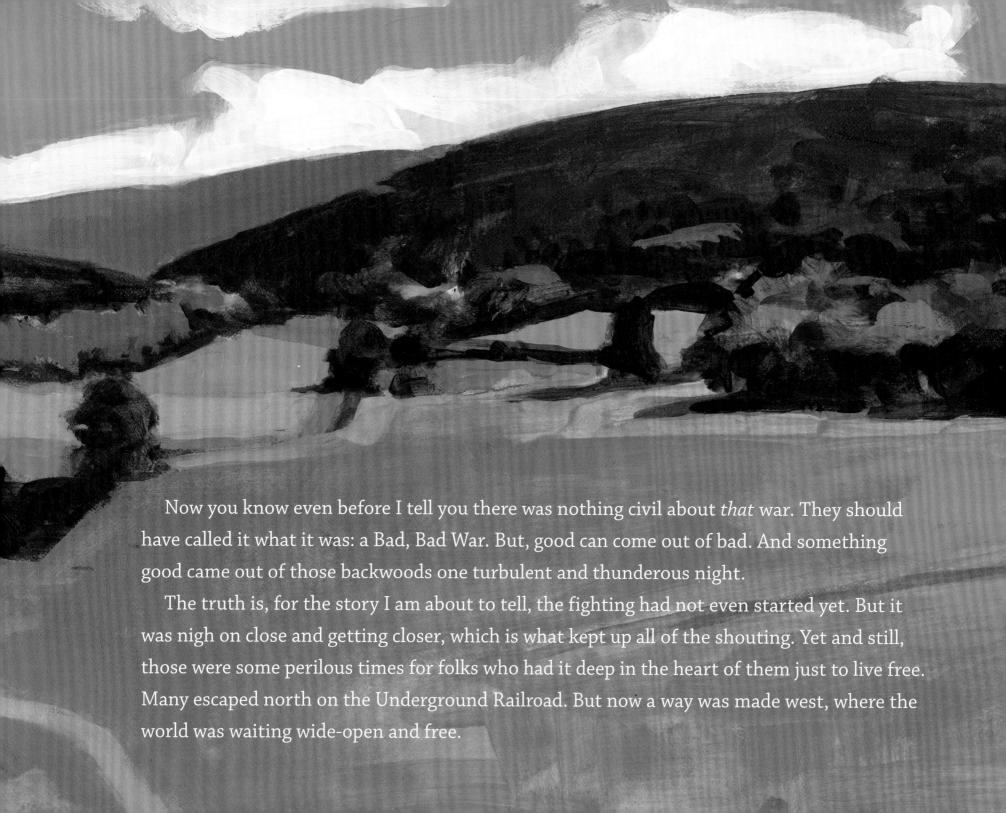

Now you know even before I tell you there was nothing civil about *that* war. They should have called it what it was: a Bad, Bad War. But, good can come out of bad. And something good came out of those backwoods one turbulent and thunderous night.

The truth is, for the story I am about to tell, the fighting had not even started yet. But it was nigh on close and getting closer, which is what kept up all of the shouting. Yet and still, those were some perilous times for folks who had it deep in the heart of them just to live free. Many escaped north on the Underground Railroad. But now a way was made west, where the world was waiting wide-open and free.

Like every other slave on Simon Plenty's plantation, John and Millicent suffered one hurt and heartbreak after another. But the worst of things was when, one by one, their parents, Samuel and Maggie, were sold away. I don't have to tell you the pain this could put on anyone, let alone a child. But long before this, Samuel and Maggie had sown the seeds of freedom in their children's minds and hearts.

Back in the long-ago days, Samuel and Maggie had told their children, "When they wanted to and could remember how, our people could fly away to freedom as free and easy as any bird. There is beauty and music in the flight of birds—listen for the song. It is a song for the soul, a dance for the heart. Their wings comb melodies from the air."

Millicent and John *had* taken to those old tales of flying. In the brightness of day, the stories seemed like fancies concocted to soothe a battered brow. Yet and still, they carried the dream with them as they toiled the fields, until it began to weave and wrap itself around them like a quilt. It began to take root in their hearts and minds. Anyone living knows it is a want and a desire so deep to human feeling, so brave to human spirit, any human heart would cry out, "Go ahead, go ahead. *Be free. Be free. Remember, oh remember, how to make yourselves free.*"

"Maybe such a time will come for you," Samuel and Maggie had told their children.

But until then, John and Millicent did what every other slave had to do on Simon Plenty's plantation: start their backbreaking labor at the first light of day and end because it was too dark to see. They worked in all weather, wet or dry, hot or cold. And Brone Sorenson, the overseer, watched over them to make sure. As they labored in the fields, John and Millicent wished and dreamed and imagined.

But this day, only one lone and mysterious bird circled overhead. Beholding such majesty with no ties or bounds to it put Sorenson in a merciless mood. Adept and ready with his cruel edged leather, he supposed he could yank the bird right out of the air. Taking right aim at that beauty, the lash split the air— light flashed across the sky. All movement and music stopped. The act created a great wrong that in time would need to be made right. "Ha, landed it." Sorenson laughed! The strange bird fell at Millicent's feet. She reached for it.

"Leave it!" he barked his ugly command.

But that night, as the full face of the moon shone wide and bright, neither child could rest, neither child did sleep. They worried and worried about the poor bird.

"Let us go to it," Millicent decided. "If just to bury it proper."

Discovering life was left in it yet, they carried it home. It was a large bird, like no other seen around these parts before. Its long, spindly legs made the children wonder how it could stand on them at all. Millicent and John only wanted to tend its wounds. With the sweet milk of human kindness and despite the risk, they determined to nurse the strange bird back to its good health. There was no turning back now.

But the next morning, more misery ripped at their hearts. John was hired away to Mr. Findlay's farm to help with the ginning. No telling how long he would be gone—five, six, seven months? The better part of a year? "You be strong, now!" John whispered to his sister.

During the day, when Millicent was in the fields, the bird slept silent, keeping to the shadows of the cabin as if he knew he had to. But at night, when she returned, its feathers, black as jet, seemed to glow like burning coals, lighting the room as though by many candles.

Standing as tall as Millicent, the bird had a wingspan that filled up the room. The cooing, warbling music it made sounded like a song of water falling down upon rocks. Millicent listened, learned its sounds and its ways. She was never frightened of it. She played games with the bird. They developed a trick: The bird, standing behind her, would stretch out its wings. From the shadow they formed, it felt to Millicent that she had grown her own wings and she could indeed fly. Now more than ever, she wished, she dreamed.

Finally, four months to the day, the ginning done, John returned home. The children were together again, but happiness was not long. Made to work a grown man's day and carry a grown man's load, John was left too tired and beaten to hold on to the desire and the dream. Secret word came to them that in one week's time John would be sold to a farm in faraway Georgia.

Now was the moment to set the dream free.

You know, fate is a gleaming star that has its own way of pointing you out and shining down on you in the form of Providence. And sometimes one's fated star can shine down and cross with the shining of another. And when those stars meet, that can make some powerful shining. Those not used to looking or expecting not to see can be blinded by that light. It was so this night. Those stars shone down on John and Millicent Wheeler. It was a matter of moments and motions.

"Fly," Millicent pleaded. But the bird stood still. "Shoo." She waved the bird on. But the bird would not move. Instead it perched and sang. Without a thought Millicent joined in. The song soared from her mouth.

While on his rounds Sorenson heard the commotion. He rushed to the Quarters. He vowed to destroy the bird once and for all. This only strengthened Millicent's resolve. She sang ever louder.

With every beat of her heart, Sorenson stepped closer until he was upon them.

"Fly," she pleaded with the bird. "Run," she called to John. And he did.

For on this night, John and his sister, Millicent, chose freedom.

With Sorenson now behind them, the mysterious bird opened its wings and lifted itself high into the air.

The wind pitched and howled. The air crackled and sizzled in flashes of light. Instinctively Millicent and John knew to follow its path. It was heading west.

And those children went running, aiming as far away as away would take them. "Run. Oh, run!" they called to each other. And they ran, oh, they ran. They ran ahead of that storm. And they never stopped running until they reached the deep places in the woods. The strong arms of the wind protected them. No search team could get to those children past that storm.

It is sometimes said that night is the shadow of a broad-winged bird, as big as the world itself comes gently and quietly soaring in on the day to swallow the daylight whole. Like freedom, night is something to wonder about.

Later folks tell of their escape through the story of a storm. They say that is all that those children left behind. They say it is a mystery the way things happened that night. Storms rose out of a calm and peaceful sky. Burdens, like souls, were lifted and carried away from hardship, affliction, or any strife. Folks say, "It was a thing to wonder about and a mystery how John and Millicent ran away so free, as sweet and easy as eating pudding."

But the truth is, they hid in the woods and pecked their way north until they reached the Missouri River. There they hitched aboard a wagon train heading for the wide-open spaces of the West. That is how they got free!

Oh, child, don't you know that is how they made themselves free!

AUTHOR'S NOTE

Telling stories helps us to make meaning and sense of the world. There is power in storytelling. At its best, a story can help to instruct, soothe, or heal. Flying is often used as a motif for healing.

Folklore is filled with myths, legends, and stories of the magic of flight. In storytelling and literature the metaphor of flight and flying is often used to set the imagination free. Many enslaved Africans used this metaphor in order to escape the misery they had to endure.

But, before I get too far ahead, it is best that I return to the beginning to fetch what must not be lost or left behind.

It was *Big Jabe* who started me on this story path. In it I imagined a multigenerational narrative of an African American family who lived in North Carolina on the fictional plantation of Simon Plenty from the 1820s to the 1880s. My goal was to create three stories meant to sit side by side, each one supporting the other's story: *Big Jabe*, *Freedom Bird*, and *Thunder Rose*.

Whereas *Big Jabe* may imply the escape to the north, *Freedom Bird* fills in the story of an escape to the west. It is specifically the story of the mother of *Thunder Rose*, Millicent MacGruder (née Wheeler), and how she went west.

And so now you know everything.

SUGGESTIONS FOR FURTHER READING

There are many fine books on this period in history. Here is a list of some that I have referenced in telling this story.

Douglass, Frederick. *Narrative of the Life of Frederick Douglass: An American Slave*. New York: Signet, 1968.

Foner, Eric. *Gateway to Freedom: The Hidden History of the Underground Railroad*. New York: W.W. Norton & Company Ltd., 2015.

Hamilton, Virginia. *The People Could Fly*. New York: Alfred A. Knopf, 1985.

Hamilton, Virginia. *Many Thousand Gone: African Americans from Slavery to Freedom*. New York: Alfred A. Knopf, 1985.

Petry, Ann. *Harriet Tubman: Conductor on the Underground Railroad*. New York: Amistad; Reprint. Revised edition, 2018.